Hot city

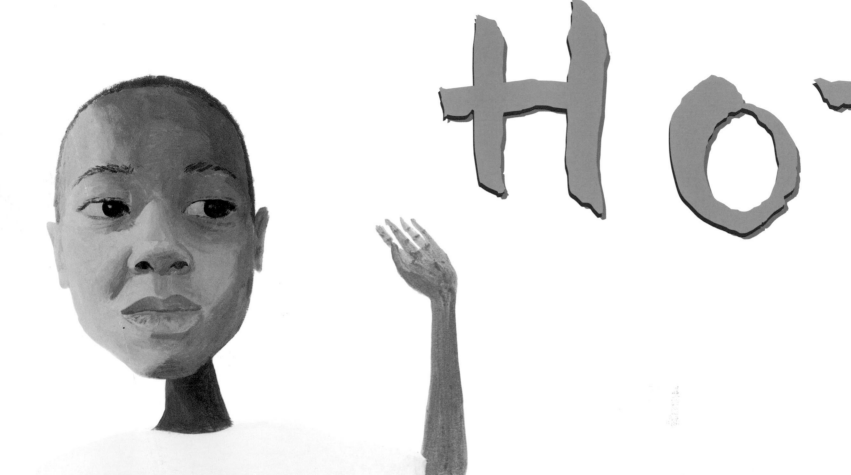

Hot

illustrated by **R. Gregory Christie**

City

by Barbara Joosse

Philomel Books
New York

PATRICIA LEE GAUCH, EDITOR

Text copyright © 2004 by Barbara Joosse. Illustrations copyright © 2004 by R. Gregory Christie.
All rights reserved. This book, or parts thereof, may not be reproduced in any form without permission in writing from the publisher,
PHILOMEL BOOKS,
a division of Penguin Young Readers Group, 345 Hudson Street, New York, NY 10014.
Philomel Books, Reg. U.S. Pat. & Tm. Off. The scanning, uploading and distribution of this book via the Internet or
via any other means without the permission of the publisher is illegal and punishable by law. Please purchase only authorized electronic editions,
and do not participate in or encourage electronic piracy of copyrighted materials. Your support of the author's rights is appreciated.
Published simultaneously in Canada. Manufactured in China by South China Printing Co. Ltd.
Designed by Semadar Megged. Text set in 22-point Triplex Bold.
The artwork was done in acrylic paint on illustration board.
Library of Congress Cataloging-in-Publication Data
Joosse, Barbara M. Hot city / by Barbara Joosse ; illustrated by R. Gregory Christie ; Patricia Lee Gauch, editor.— 1st ed.   p. cm.
Summary: Mimi and her little brother Joe escape from home and the city's summer heat to read and dream about princesses
and dinosaurs in the cool, quiet library.
[1. City and town life—Fiction. 2. Libraries—Fiction. 3. Summer—Fiction. 4. Brothers and sisters—Fiction. 5. African Americans—Fiction.]
I. Christie, Gregory, 1971–, ill. II. Gauch, Patricia Lee, ed.
III. Title. PZ7.J7435 Hm 2004 [E]—dc21 2002001254
ISBN 0-399-23640-6
3 5 7 9 10 8 6 4 2

*For Joe, who loves books
and my daughter.* —BJ

*For Sandra Green, Steven Green, and Ajamu Hooks.
Thank you for your friendship and the many summertime
days spent together on Jackson Avenue.* —RGC

Me and Joe on the front porch steps,
cement steps, hot as a fry pan,
sizzlin'.
And my own sweet self?
That's what's cookin'.

"Hey, Mimi," says Joe. He's my little brother.
"Whatcha wanna do?"

"Nothin'," I say.

"Nothin'?" he says.

"Uh-huh."

But Joe can't do nothin'. Oh, no. He's got jumps in his skin.
"Hey, Mimi," says Joe. "Let's us spy on the blah blah ladies."

"Nyuh-uh," I say.

"Mrs. Parker's wearin' a fancy dress. Like a princess, Mimi . . ."

Inside.
"Blah blah," says Mrs. Parker, flouncin' her dress.
"Blah blah blah," says Mama, fannin' her face.
"Blah blah," says Aunt Phyl.

Mama sees me.
"Oooh, sweet girl!
Pour that ice tea, would you, honey?
And Joe, pass us some cookies."
We do-for Mama and the blah blah ladies,
then slip out, slow and easy.

We walk.
Sweat runs like a river—
'cross my face, down my back,
fillin' me up.

The snow-cone man rings his bell at us.
"Mimi?" asks Joe, his eyes big as moons.

Two snow cones.
Princess pink for me.
Dinosaur green for Joe.

We lick fast,
but not fast enough.

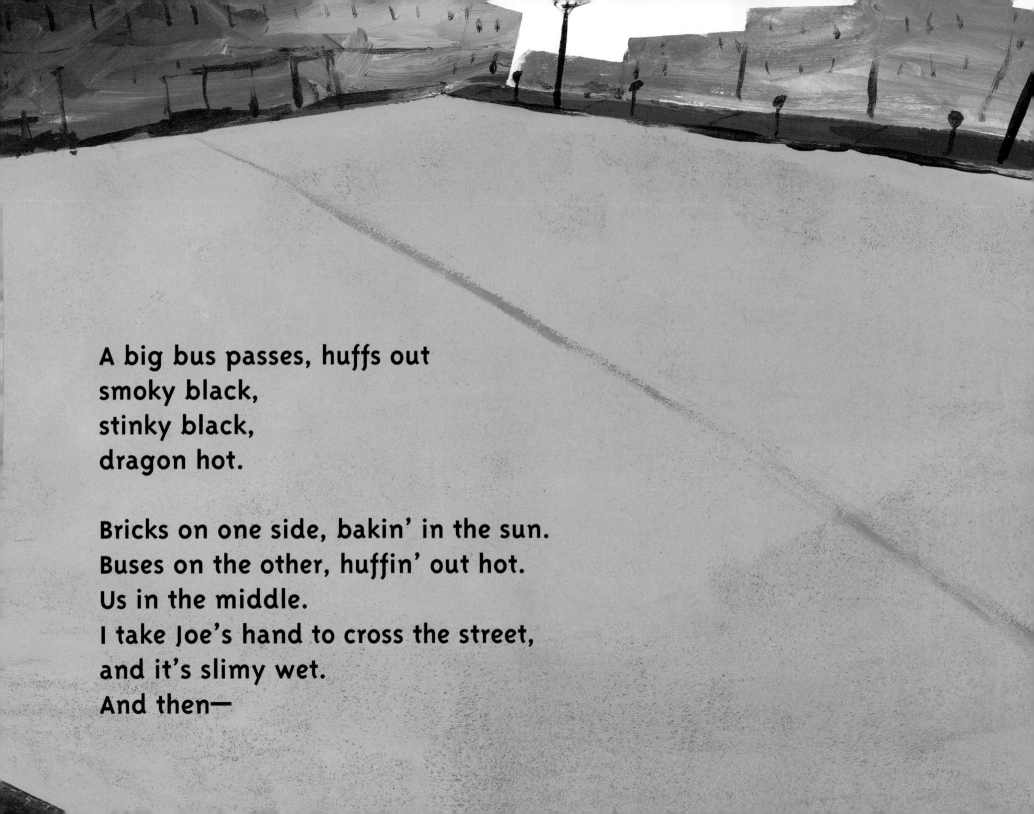

A big bus passes, huffs out
smoky black,
stinky black,
dragon hot.

Bricks on one side, bakin' in the sun.
Buses on the other, huffin' out hot.
Us in the middle.
I take Joe's hand to cross the street,
and it's slimy wet.
And then—

In the coooool library,
I go where I want,
so I take myself to the Princess shelf.

Joe goes to Dinosaurs.

We take our time,
pickin'
slow.

In the library, I sit where I want,
so I plop down in a big old chair,
smooth and cool,
like a throne.

I turn the pages of my book slow,
like a princess.
I rub my finger on the gold-sparkle edge,
like a princess.
I look at the gowns and then—

Me and Joe look down at the city,
sizzlin' hot.
There's people out there,
sweatin' out rivers.
There's buses out there,
huffin' out hot.

Still hot out there.
Cool in here.

"Mimi," Joe says, grinnin'.
"It's good we came. Isn't it."
Joe sticks out his chest like he's
King Stuff.

"It's good," I say.